LOVE'S
A
SWEET

LOVE'S A SWEET

BY Clyde Watson

ILLUSTRATED BY Wendy Watson

VIKING

VIKING
Published by the Penguin Group
Penguin Putnam Inc., 345 Hudson Street, New York, New York 10014, U.S.A.
Penguin Books Ltd, 27 Wrights Lane, London W8 5TZ, England
Penguin Books Australia Ltd, Ringwood, Victoria, Australia
Penguin Books Canada Ltd, 10 Alcorn Avenue, Toronto, Ontario, Canada M4V 3B2
Penguin Books (N.Z.) Ltd, 182-190 Wairau Road, Auckland 10, New Zealand

Penguin Books Ltd, Registered Offices: Harmondsworth, Middlesex, England

First published in 1998 by Viking, a member of Penguin Putnam Books for Young Readers.

1 3 5 7 9 10 8 6 4 2

LIBRARY OF CONGRESS CATALOGING-IN-PUBLICATION DATA
Watson, Clyde.
Love's a sweet / by Clyde Watson ; illustrated by Wendy Watson.
p. cm.
Summary: a collection of short poems and rhymes, illustrated with animal characters, showing the ups and downs of love in everyday situations.
ISBN 0-670-83453-X (hc)
1. Love—Juvenile poetry. 2. Children's poetry, American.
3. American poetry. [1. Love—Poetry.] I. Watson, Wendy, ill.
II. Title. PS3573.A8485L68 1998 811'.54—dc21 98-14273 CIP AC

Printed in Hong Kong
Set in Bookman

This book is dedicated to
Roseminna McLeod Watson
who waited . . .
& waited . . .
& WAITED for it . . .
and finally,
HERE IT IS!

Love's a sweet no money can buy
And a riddle that none can explain;
More precious, 'tis said, than emeralds or gold
And yet as common as rain.

My sunshine in the morning,
Sweet music to my ear,
Merry jewel of my heart,
My child, keep you near.

Every time I think of you
My heart speeds up a beat or two.
In all the world, as you might guess, I
Long to hear just one word:
Yes!

Charley came for breakfast,
Charley came for tea,
Charley came for dinner,
Footloose & fancy-free.

Charley spilled the coffee,
Charley spilled the tea,
Charley broke the dinner plate,
And all for the love of me.

Kisses, kisses,
As many as you please,
One for your chin
And eleven for your knees,

Forty for your fingers,
And fifty for your toes,
A googolplex and eighty-eight
For the tippity-tip of your nose.

Mister Right,
My love-at-first-sight,
So new & handsome & clever;
The last time about
Just didn't work out
But this time it's love forever!

Jesse is a thumbprint,
A wee little dot,
An angel when he's sleeping
And a devil when he's not.

Hey ho, my dearie-o,
And off to town she goes,
With ninety-nine pennies stuffed into a purse
To buy her some fine new clothes.

Red to match her rosy cheeks,
Hazel to match her eyes,
Gold to match her loving heart
And blue to match the skies.

A pocket full of promises,
A new one every minute.
But turn his pocket inside out
And look: there's nothing in it!

Love, hate, joy, & sorrow
All rolled into one,
And nary a way
To sort it out
Before the day is done.

Old head, wise eyes,
Dreams so far away,
Dear hands, deserving rest,
At the end of the day;

Let me plump your pillows up
And comb your hair so fine,
And hold your hand until you sleep
As once you held mine.

Sweep the bread crumbs under the rug,
There's company coming for tea:
And when he finds out how *you* keep house
Then maybe he'll marry *me!*

A penny for your thoughts,
A nickel for your wishes,
And all the tea in China
If, for once, *you* wash the dishes!

Dearling darling love of mine,
You're my truest valentine;
Of all the loves I ever knew
I only ever wanted you.

And now we're old & bent & gray,
We still hold hands & laugh & say:

Dearling darling love of mine,
You're my truest valentine;
Of all the loves I ever knew
I only ever wanted you.

Oh once I had a baby
And Georgia was her name.
Now she's all grown up
But she's my baby just the same.

Jack & Jenny got into a quarrel,
Nobody knows what for:
Jenny called Jack a slobberchops,
And Jack called Jenny a bore;

But when they were done with the shouting of names
And the crying & slamming of doors,
They hugged & kissed & made it all up
And vowed they would fight no more.

Johnny O'Hare,
He sleeps bare,
His wife wears a nightie at night;
But when they tuck
The covers up
They're both just right.

Cats & dogs &
Hammer & tongs &
Never the two shall agree:
Day in & day out
They argue & shout
Yet they're happy as they can be.

I love Kate & she loves me,
Oh, what a perfect pair we'll be!
One in tails & one in tatters:
So what? Love's the thing that matters.

First there was one,
Now there are two,
Lickety-split comes three:
A new little nubbin
That kicks in the night,
Old Daddy Longlegs & me.

Crazy crazy lean & lazy
Lies in bed till noon,
Leaves the teacups in the woods,
Eats soup without a spoon,

Wears his tee-shirt inside out,
The same one every day,
Combs his hair but twice a year:
I love him anyway.

Farmer, fisher,
Carpenter, clerk,
Teacher, trucker,
Jack-of-all-work,

Mountain climber,
Mathematician,
Lion tamer,
Electrician,

Singer, dancer,
Brewer, baker,
Poet, painter,
Music maker,

Actor, astronaut,
Gymnast, cook,
Sailor, senator,
Millionaire, crook.

Come here, come near,
Come close, my dear,
And let me whisper
In your ear:
My pippin, my poppet,
My pumpkin, my dove,
My honey, my darling,
My own pretty love.

Up & away to Ballston Beach
To feast on love & kisses,
And when we come back
You can tip your hat
And call us Mister & Missus!

Bye lo bye, my midnight baby,
Stars are in the sky,
Go to sleep, & the morning sun
Will wake you by and by.